*I don't want an intellectual education. Knowledge ruins our youth."*
–Adolf Hitler

# ACKNOWLEDGMENTS

I thank my father, Günter, and my mother, Helga, whose willingness to visit painful events in their memories never ceased to astound me. Without them there would be no story. I also want to thank Helmut's family for allowing me to share his part of the story. Over the past fifteen years I've had many people help me make this novel possible: Alexander Weinstein who helped me through a first version of the manuscript when I still had much to learn and who instilled in me the belief that I could one day become a novelist; my writing buddies Diane, Susan and Dave who've read several versions of this story over the years; the Stadtarchiv Solingen for sharing my hometown's history; and Sara from Yellow Bird Editors for pointing out what was still missing and helping me arrive at a meaningful end. And finally my husband and best friend, Ben, who's stood by me and endured endless discussions, the occasional tears and many readings.

BASED ON TRUE EVENTS

# PROLOGUE

What made me do it? Even now, more than seventy years later, I cannot say. Not exactly, at least.

Oh, I do have an inkling. So let me explain.

I was the middle of three boys, my brother, Hans, just about a year older, my younger brother, Siegfried, eight years my junior. In our German home my father ruled and we obeyed, his box to the ear quicker than the strike of a cobra. Yet, we knew our place, each of us bonded within to our family, with homemade sweetbread, butter and red current jam on Sunday mornings, and the conviction that life would always continue as it had.

That is until the war started and my father went away. From then on, as months turned to years and life grew into the monstrous chore of survival, I forgot my good German manners, my obedience. I became someone else, a person I sometimes didn't recognize, a being that fought and scraped like the lowest animal.

Until that fateful spring in 1945, I never realized what 'home' meant and what I'd do to keep it in my heart. How deep Hitler's evil reached. How it changed the way I looked at the world and forced me to make an impossible choice.

Anymore, my memory plays tricks. But though I struggle to keep my day-to-day life straight, I clearly remember the day everything started.

I remember when we were ordered to die for the Fatherland.

# SOLINGEN, GERMANY, MARCH 5, 1945

I sat on my hands to keep them from freezing when our teacher, Herr Leimer, entered. After the citywide bombing last November when just about everything in Solingen had shut down, I'd finally managed to get back into a vocational school that accepted new students.

Leimer was old as dirt and had been pulled from retirement after all the real teachers had joined the war. It was March and our classroom, windows carefully plastered with assorted vinyl, cardboard and tarpaper, was as gloomy and cold as the frozen landscape outside.

Like my classmates, I wore a coat and a wool hat Mother had knitted from an old sweater. You could see puffs of breath rise from every desk. People coughed and sniffed, our noses red and dripping. Frustrated about the stiffness in my fingers, I had been opening and closing my fists because technical drawing was my favorite subject.

But instead of going to the board and suggesting a quick-draw to warm up, Leimer repeatedly cleared his throat. His cheeks, rugged from age and too many cold nights—or as some rumored, too much drink—burned unusually red.

When the shuffling of chairs and bodies finally ceased, I forgot my icy hands. The old man looked as if he'd fall over any second. He even swayed a bit. Still, he didn't speak. Instead he looked at us with his watery blue eyes, holding everyone's gaze until the chair shuffling resumed and everyone began to whisper.

That's when Leimer raised his arms and the room turned as silent as a graveyard.

"Boys," he said. "I was asked to tell you…" Leimer's voice choked a little. "You've been summoned for another muster. Let me read what it says." He labored to unfold an official looking document, his hands bony and covered with bluish veins.

"Every man, born 1928 or 1929, must report for muster." He paused, his breath loud in the stillness. "If found fit for battle, your orders are as follows: Travel to *Marburg* by next Monday, March 12 and find the office of the Hitler youth." The paper sank. With it Leimer's voice. "That gives you a week. But first you have to report for muster to update your papers. Everything else will be explained there."

I scratched my jaw and took a look around the room. Had I heard right? I'd been mustered last fall and they told us then that we were deferred. I mean I was barely sixteen, some of us still fifteen.

This couldn't be happening. Not now. I'd been sure the war would be over soon. Of course, nobody said it out loud, but at home people whispered of certain defeat. Last December when we'd met the horse soldier, he'd insisted the end was near.

A tremble went through me, starting at my toes and moving up and out through my limbs. I wanted to hurl my pencil at Leimer.

"How will we get to Marburg?" somebody asked.

"Where's Marburg? Are we all going?" Excited voices filled the room.

Leimer raised both arms. "Silence." The chatter subsided reluctantly. "There is no official transport to Marburg. It's maybe two hundred kilometers southeast. You must find the way yourself. Look for a truck or try catching a train. Most likely you'll have to walk."

"Why do we have to go now?" Paul Mans was still as small as last summer when the officer had slapped him around during muster. I was sure he dreaded another visit. So did I.

"The Führer needs everyone's help." Leimer hesitated as if he wanted to say more. But then he simply shook his head.

"What about uniforms?" somebody said.

"And weapons?" another boy yelled.

Leimer frowned. "I assume you'll receive everything when

you get there. Class dismissed."

The room erupted in chatter, voices in various levels of development, deep baritones, mixed with scratchy adolescents. I watched Rolf Schlüter who always bragged and shoved people around. You were either in the Rolf Schlüter club or you weren't. I definitely wasn't.

Right now Rolf was surrounded by a throng of eager listeners. They all leaned in close while Rolf was explaining his strategy. "It's easy, you'll see. If we all do our part we'll be there in no time."

Funny, I thought as I carefully placed the pencil stub in my pocket, Rolf is good at taking credit for other people's work.

Honestly, I couldn't believe how these boys could be excited. Had they not been around for the past five and a half years? Their chattering was getting on my nerves and all I wanted to do was leave—get away from them and their foolishness.

"What about you, Günter?" Rolf looked at me expectantly.

I swallowed a curse, forcing my expression into neutral. At least I hoped it looked that way. "I'll see if my friend, Helmut, is going. We'll head out together."

"Come on. Get your friend to join us. We're meeting in *Höhscheid* after the muster."

"Why there?" I asked, immediately regretting it. Now he'd think I was interested.

"Dieter says military convoys pass through all the time. We can catch a ride real easy."

How confident he sounded. "I'll try to make it, but I'm going to wait for Helmut," I said.

"What do you mean *try*?" Dieter asked. "You should be more enthusiastic. Didn't you hear the Führer *needs* us? This will be fun."

I attempted a smile though I wanted to shake my head. How could Dieter consider this war fun? Even a blind man could see that Germany was lost.

"Find your own way then," Rolf said. "But you'll look pretty stupid arriving days late while we catch ourselves some Russians." As if on cue, his friends laughed.

"My brother knows somebody in the *Partei*," one of Rolf's friends volunteered.

"My uncle is a major. He might know something," another

boy chimed in.

How could these brothers and uncles be home when my father had been gone for years? Four years and ten months to be exact. And my brother, Hans, had left last fall. I didn't know much, but I knew that joining the war wasn't a smart idea. *You'd do what your father and Hans are doing. You'd be one of them.*

Standing back, I watched the group. Despite his strong words, Rolf looked small among his classmates. Several inches shorter than his friends, his voice didn't carry as if it were snuffed out by the bodies around him.

"I bet we'll arrive early," Rolf said. "Who is coming with me?" All hands in the group shot up. "Let's go and prepare. See you at muster." He stormed out, followed by his buddies.

I stayed behind along with Paul, who was slowly packing his bag. Herr Leimer still sat at his desk on the podium. He seemed to have aged overnight. I wanted to ask him what he was going to do now that the class had been dissolved, but then I remembered the muster. I couldn't be late, especially when it took forever to get there. The roads were still buried in rubble.


That afternoon I saw my classmates at the old elementary school where the military had set up another office. The other location had been destroyed during November's attacks. We all had to strip again and stand in line.

The commandeering officer looked grim as we stood shivering in the frigid air. This muster was even shorter than last time, the ancient doctor hardly looking at us. We all received marching orders to Marburg.

On my way home, I went to see Helmut. I knew immediately that he'd been to muster as well. His beaky nose looked even longer than usual and his cheeks were pale.

"I thought you might be stopping by," he said, leading the way to his room. He lived with his mother in a tiny white and black half-timber house in the old neighborhood of *Unnersberg* and had to lower his head in the doorframe.

"I'm not going. At least not immediately," I said as I plopped on Helmut's bed and told him about my lousy morning. "Remember the soldiers we saw in December? They said we should wait it out. The war will be over soon."

"I don't want to go either," said Helmut. "But we can't stay here. You know what they do if we get caught." His voice quivered as he sagged on a wooden chair by the window. He was usually pretty laid back, but this afternoon his forehead shone with sweat despite the chilly room.

"Of course, we can't stay, but we don't have to go to Marburg quickly. We could take it slow and wait. They said we should *try* to be there by Monday. How will they know who is going and how long it takes? I bet, they just estimate."

"You mean we hide?"

"For a while. See how things develop."

"What if someone checks our papers?" He got back up and began to pace around the room. "I'm not telling my mother. She'll go crazy with worry."

"She'll go crazy either way." I pushed away the thought of telling my own mother. "We could have *problems* and take much longer. Maybe I hurt myself. Or we get lost."

"You don't want to meet this Rolf?"

"No way."

Helmut grinned. "He sounds like an idiot."

"I'll see if we have a map. And food."

"Let's meet tonight around seven and be ready to go," Helmut said. "In case they're watching."

Sadly, it was true. One never knew who was trustworthy. With the deterioration of the country, hunger and desperation moved into homes and some figured a method to more rations was snitching for the SS or Gestapo.

I hurried home along the inky road, carefully picking my way. We hadn't had street lanterns in five and a half years, the city cloaked in darkness to hide from air attacks. Obviously, that strategy wasn't working because by now most German cities had been bombed.

With every step, the knot in my stomach expanded. I had to tell Mother. She'd already seen my father and brother leave for duty. Now it was my turn.

Determined to remain calm, I entered the kitchen and longingly looked at the scrubbed table. No pot sat on the stove. We barely ever had enough food to cook something warm these days.

I tossed my hat and gloves into the corner and called, "I'm home."

"You're late," Mother said, emerging from her bedroom with a patchwork-darned sock in one hand. She was a small woman, no more than five feet and I had the sudden impulse of hugging her to my chest. Of course, I did no such thing. I just stood there with my arms glued to my side. "I have cornbread and a bit of jam." She rummaged in the breadbox, the hollow sound echoing my stomach. "Better sit while you eat."

My belly growled as I slumped on the bench across from her. I was hungry, but then I was not. Had she heard? I searched Mother's face for clues, but she showed the usual strained face from years of holding together her fears.

I forced air through my throat. "I've been drafted." How weird that sounded.

The darned sock dropped on the table. "What do you mean?"

"We got mustered a second time and I'm ordered to report to Marburg."

"What? Today?"

I nodded, hoping my voice remained strong. "I'm supposed to go to Marburg on my own. My entire class does. Helmut, too. I've got a week." I swallowed the last of the bread. The crumbs stuck in my throat and I gulped down a glass of water. I got up, keeping my lips pressed tight. That's how Hans had acted when he left.

"But you're barely sixteen." Mother's eyes were dark with tears, her small hands holding on the edge of the table. "Do they want to kill us all? You have to be careful, Günter. Promise me."

I nodded, resisting the urge to climb onto her lap and bury my head.

"*Mutter*, listen." I sat back down and took her fingers in mine. "I…we've decided we won't go straight there. We'll take a really long time. We'll go slowly, walk around in circles. You know what they said…the war should be over pretty soon."

"But we don't know when." Mother squeezed my fingers. "You *must* be vigilant. The SS…they'll shoot you on the spot if they even suspect—"

"Don't worry, we'll make it," I said, wishing my voice sounded more convincing—to her, and to myself. I straightened abruptly and headed to my room. Time to pack.

"Will you see Father and Hans?" My little brother,

Siegfried, hovered in the doorframe. He was only eight and seemed tiny to me, a latecomer surprise to our family.

I hurried over and kneeled in front of him. "There are lots of men out there, but I'll definitely look for them." How could I explain to my eight-year old brother that I had no intention of following my father and brother? *Traitor.* They were out there fighting a war that was long lost and what was I going to do?

Siegfried leaned his cheek against my shoulder. "Will you write?"

I squinted my eyes shut to keep them from leaking and patted his back as an answer.

# DAY ONE

It was dark when I snuck out of the house. Mother was tearful but quiet, clutching Siegfried to her chest. I swallowed repeatedly, the knot in my throat the size of a soccer ball. All the words I'd wanted to say didn't come. All I could think of were my burning eyes and my damp palms until I thought I'd choke. Had father and Hans felt the same when they'd marched off? I abruptly turned and closed the door.

It was an unusually cold night for early March, the ground frozen solid. Helmut waited at the corner, his breath steaming in the air. A half-moon colored the sky in burned orange and purple. Scattered clouds threw shadows across our path.

We walked silently, each carrying a small sack with a set of extra clothes, a blanket, some bread and a few potatoes. It was hard to comprehend we'd not go home tonight or any night soon.

I hadn't found a map, so we headed south into the woods. Somehow, we'd have to find road signs and watch the sun for direction. Leaves rustled underfoot and a frigid wind blew. We'd hiked the *Wupper River* hills a thousand times, the landscape as familiar as my backyard. I'd never realized how much I'd loved it here. How I'd taken things for granted.

"You all right?" I said to distract myself.

"Sure."

"You don't sound *sure*."

Helmut didn't answer.

"Why aren't you talking?" I couldn't keep the anger from

my voice.

"What about?"

"Idiot."

Suddenly, Helmut stopped and hurled his pack to the ground. "Who are you calling an idiot? Have you thought what happens if they catch us? Everyone is heading to Marburg. What will they do if we don't show up?"

"We just have to hide. If anyone asks, we say we got lost."

"What if we're wrong? How do you know the war will be over soon? I mean it's been going on for five and half years. What if it continues and they'll find out we..." Helmut lowered his voice. "We'll get executed."

"Shut up. The way you're going, we'll be dead in ten minutes." I wanted to smack Helmut in the nose. "I don't know what's going to happen, but I know that I don't want to go. People are dying everywhere. Everyone..." I swallowed to push away the thought of my brother and father, "is getting killed. This is stupid."

"I say we go close to Marburg. And then wait."

"Wait for what?" I scratched my forehead. "For the SS or the Russians to find us? Sit in the bushes and watch the action?"

Helmut remained silent.

"We should stay in the area and go where there're fewer people. We can always head to Marburg later."

Helmut didn't answer, but he picked up his bag and began to walk.

The trees grew denser and darker as pines and cedars mixed with oaks and beeches. We found shelter in an old hunting stand about six kilometers from home. The small box, built on twenty-foot poles overlooked a field, was one of thousands sprinkling the landscape. Not daring to make a fire, we huddled in the corner, the wind claiming free reign through the open window.

I couldn't sleep, nor could I feel my toes. It was early morning, the hour before dawn when thoughts of hopelessness and doubt whisper. Dew soaked my hair and blanket. I tried pulling my coat across my knees, but it was too short. I'd grown again over the winter.

Above me, branches moved like giant fingers. Something rustled on the ground below, the sounds magnified by the darkness. The knitted gloves Mother had given me allowed too much airflow, so I stuck my hands between my legs. I longed for my bed, the familiar sounds of home, and my mother. I dozed, but sleep refused to come.

Helmut had a point. What if we were wrong and the war continued much longer? Never mind the handful of soldiers we'd met who whispered of certain defeat. Who knew what was true? All we heard came through the radio, the barrage of announcements, the constant flyers. Not that I listened anymore—at least not on purpose.

What if we were stopped by a patrol? Or we ran into Russians or Americans? We had no weapons and no training. Not even enough to eat to last a couple of days.

I shivered.

At dawn, it began to drizzle. I looked over the fields, trying to decide on a direction. Two deer grazed below, beautiful and out of reach. Helmut was leaning back, his mouth relaxed in sleep, his wool cap covering one eye.

I punched my friend in the arm. "We better go."

"Let me sleep," Helmut mumbled, turning in search of a more comfortable position. Unable to find it, he opened his eyes. "*Scheiße*, I'm freezing."

"Get your lazy butt moving then." I was in a rotten mood. Helmut was capable of sleeping anywhere, day or night, while my own mind refused to shut off.

Heads low, we trudged into the countryside. The land rolled in soft hills and wide valleys, sprinkled with forests and open spaces, and dotted with an occasional farm or village. The wetness softened our steps but crept beneath our clothes. We walked carefully, avoiding streets and houses, jumping off the road as soon as we heard a sound.

Sometimes, we found a barn filled with straw or hay and crept inside after dark. It was easier to find or steal a bit from a farm. While most farmers had to deliver their harvest to the cause, they always seemed to have reserves. After all, it was easier to grow and hide food when you had land and outbuildings.

# DAY SEVEN

Hard to believe we'd slogged around for a week. Helmut and I had been friends since elementary school, but I was growing tired of his company. I knew he felt the same by the way he squinted at me. We hardly spoke and when we did, we mumbled some words, each encased in his own misery.

"I wonder when we can go home," Helmut said as we walked along a narrow trail. Ferns sprouted, their rolled stalks unfolding through last year's layer of leaves. The forest felt empty, void of anything edible except for the animals we couldn't catch. A ray of sun appeared, adding sharp colors but no warmth to the afternoon. What did I expect? It was only the middle of March.

I'd had the same thought, but kept my mouth shut. By hiding and avoiding others, we had cut ourselves off from any news. We ran around blind while somewhere south, the Americans were creeping closer. In the east, the Russian Army was moving toward Berlin.

What if *Solingen* had been bombed again? What if something had happened to our families?

Last November the Brits had flown a weekend attack, leveling the city. Downtown had burned for a week and when we'd gone to take a look a few weeks later, white sheets fluttered where bodies needed pickup. Along the sidewalks the dead had been stacked like cordwood, the stench of decomposing bodies a toxic cloud taking our breath.

Ever since I'd avoided thinking about the carnage, but

now that we were away, I found not knowing was torture. I pulled off my cap and scratched my head. Everything itched.

"Let's rehearse again and make sure we say the same thing." I couldn't help myself thinking about being caught. It was as if a thundercloud followed me ready to strike.

"We're going to Marburg?" Helmut volunteered.

"Maybe we should say we got turned around. Lost our way in the woods."

"We better say I turned my ankle. Who's going to believe we're lost for a week?"

"All right. Fine." I couldn't keep the irritation from my voice.

"If we'd followed *my* idea, we wouldn't have to constantly think of different excuses. We'd just wait in the wings."

I bit my lip. Maybe Helmut was right. But the thought of going south and getting near the very people who would execute us if they knew made me shudder. "Let's wait a little longer."

Helmut sighed, a deep rumbling sound. "You think the others arrived?"

"They might already be shooting people." I imagined Rolf with a rifle, his face covered with mud, taking aim at an invisible enemy. I thought of Paul Mans, the small boy who always seemed afraid even in class. Doubt crept up in me, and I abruptly left the trail.

"Where are you going?" Helmut yelled after me.

I shrugged and scratched my neck where the wool coat had left a circle of raw skin. I had to distract myself. My armpits reeked and my crotch itched. We'd soon pick up lice or some other vermin if we didn't wash. But that wasn't what bugged me. The aimless wandering was driving me crazy. Helmut's frown was driving me crazy. Worst of all were my own indecision and doubts.

With a sigh, I thought of my bathtub. Even if I had to haul water and warm it on the stove, it had been pure luxury compared to living in the woods.

"You want to wash?" Helmut's expression was incredulous as if I'd suggested flying to Africa. Helmut dipped a forefinger into the water. "Liquid ice."

I ignored him and stared at the stream that gurgled across moss-covered rocks. This early in the year, the water was knee-deep. Light reflected off its surface in brilliant colors. Ordinarily, I loved all bodies of water, had built plenty of dams in the creek in front of our house. But I'd only gone swimming when it was hot. I pulled off my coat and sweater, unbuttoned shirt and pants, shed shoes and socks, toes curling against the cold dampness of a long winter.

The air pierced my skin. Goose bumps spread. Helmut didn't move.

"Are you going to watch or what?"

"Fine." With a sigh Helmut tossed down his bag and tore off his jacket.

I turned my back and waded into the stream, splashing myself. "Damn, it's freezing." My feet were numb, making it impossible to keep my balance. I slipped and took a dive.

My ears filled with ice, my lungs bucked. Now I understood what 'mind-numbing' cold' meant. Even after two winters with no coal, I'd never frozen like this. I frantically pulled my legs beneath and straightened with a splash.

Helmut was down to his underwear, his lips blue. "We don't have any towels," he stuttered. His collarbones stood out, his ribs lined in perfect order below like the keys of a piano. Why had I never noticed? Before the war we used to go swimming to the public pool. A lifetime ago.

So, why go on? Why not lie down right here, right now? Or better yet, march to the next Hitler Youth office to turn ourselves in. I couldn't answer that question. All I knew was that I'd continue as long as I could walk. I had to believe a new life waited somewhere beyond the horizon. What was another day or week after five and a half years?

"I can't wait to take a real bath again," I said as I rubbed myself down with my shirt, pulling the spare underpants from my bag. A thousand needles pricked my feet and legs and, had it not been for the hollowness in my middle, I'd felt refreshed.

"Let's go," I said as soon as Helmut was dressed.

My urge to move was greater than my need to rest.

# DAY TEN

Ten days had passed and we were getting into a routine. Every time we reached a road, we watched and listened for several minutes before crossing, only to disappear into the next thicket. With the forest virtually void of food, farms and fields were the only place to score: a handful of potatoes or rutabagas, sorrel and half-rotten apples, a few soggy grains. Not daring to make a fire, we chewed our few finds raw.

We hiked cross-country until we came upon a small, well-kept farm far back from the road. I scanned the grounds for signs of political expression, a swastika or the German flag.

There were none. The house stood quietly. Not even a rooster crowed.

"Let's ask for food," Helmut said.

"You think it's safe?" I scanned the windows of the farmhouse, imagining eyes behind the curtains. The home had red brick walls and clay shingles. The modest barn next to it showed two low-rising stalls. Nobody was in sight.

We rehearsed quickly… on the way to Marburg, got lost, needing supplies to get there.

I knew Helmut was afraid by the way his upper lip trembled. Just in the last two days I'd noticed my own legs turn shaky. It was like walking on half-cooked spaghetti. My stomach hurt most of the time, and I had trouble sleeping even though the nights had been warmer.

"You want to ask?" I whispered.

"Maybe we should wait till dark and look for something to steal."

"We need to eat," I hissed. Anger reared inside me like a vicious animal, another side effect of starvation. Yet, I didn't move either.

"We better find out how many people live here," Helmut said, settling himself against a tree stump.

Out of nowhere a dog the size of a German shepherd raced straight at us, black fur bristling. It growled and showed impressive white fangs.

"*Guter Hund*," I whispered, feeling my leg muscles tighten, wondering if we could afford to turn our backs without being eaten for lunch.

The dog drew closer, paws silent on the packed dirt, its snarl vicious. As I began to tremble, Helmut cried, "Move slowly and climb the tree."

An old man materialized in the entrance of the farmhouse and pointed a rifle at us. "What do you want?"

"I wonder if you could…" Helmut said.

"Spit it out, boy. I don't have all day."

"We're hungry…and unarmed," I offered. That was technically untrue, because I never went anywhere without my pocketknife. My knees remained frozen in place.

"Up to no good, are you?" The man waved the rifle and took a step closer.

"We just wanted to ask for something to eat," Helmut said. "We better go."

"Not so fast. Come out of that bush and show yourselves." Had the farmer's voice softened or was I hallucinating?

"Hungry, eh?" he said as we slowly approached.

I kept one eye on the dog, which had stopped growling, the other on the barrel of the gun. I felt Helmut next to me and considered giving him a sign. But whether to run or advance was anybody's guess.

"Come here, Rudi." The dog trotted to the old man, tail wagging.

"I can see you haven't eaten in a while." The old man's gaze came to rest on our mud-covered boots. "A shame what this country is coming to." He shook his head and walked inside. I hesitated and looked at Helmut.

"What are you waiting for? Come in," the farmer said. "Take off your shoes."

The kitchen looked worn like the man's knobby hands, but the oak table was polished clean. The man set his rifle in the corner by the sink. "Let's see what we have," he mumbled as we halted halfway into the room. "Sit, boy."

Was the old fellow talking to his dog or us?

The man rustled around his cupboards. "Sit down, boys." He nodded at the table.

We sank on chairs across from each other, my throat dry and my stomach knotting with hunger and worry.

In front of us paradise unfolded: dark rye bread, butter, cheese, homemade jam and dried sausage. It was impossible to tear my eyes away. Helmut gulped saliva.

"So, who are you?" The farmer's eyes, sunken within the folds of lose skin, were hard to read.

We're in hiding, I wanted to say. We're running away from the war.

I sighed with relief, hearing Helmut say, "I'm Helmut. This is my friend, Günter. We're on our way to Marburg to enlist."

The farmer studied our faces. "How old are you?"

"Sixteen," we both said at the same time.

The kitchen turned silent. Somewhere in the corner, wood settled in a stove. I was trying to breathe shallowly. My hands shook under the table. All I could think of was the food in front of me, and our lie hovering like an evil ghost in the kitchen.

Strawberries, my brain announced as a whiff of jam slammed into my nostrils.

"...better be careful?" The old man's eyes were on me.

"What?" I said.

The old man shook his head as he sagged on a bench next to us. "I said you boys are much too young to fight. You must be careful."

I nodded slowly, watching the old man's expression. Things sat between us. Unspoken things, yet I was no longer afraid.

I reached for a slice of bread and forgot our misery.

The man watched in silence as we stuffed ourselves. At last I leaned back with a sigh. We'd said little, the old farmer's face relaxed, his eyes twinkling beneath the shadows of humungous gray brows.

"You can sleep in the barn if you want. Just stay out of sight during the day."

I nodded, pulling my gaze away from the bread. My stomach bulged and yet I wanted to eat more.

"I'll give you breakfast and something for the road tomorrow." The old farmer nodded and straightened with a grunt. "Promise me to be careful."

I attempted a smile and shook my head. The man sounded like Mother. Better not think about home. Not now, not any time soon.

But when we sank into the hay, which smelled fresh and felt warm to the touch, and the wind's whispers lulled me away, my thoughts wandered to my parents and Hans, and how they were all scattered. I longed to be with them.

In the beginning, I'd counted the number of days: 192 days since my father left, 33 days since Hans had been drafted, 97 days since I'd last eaten a decent meal. Now, five years later, I counted in years.

Most of the time I didn't count at all.

# DAY THIRTEEN

We stayed two nights, helping the old man with cleanup, stacking wood and straw. On the thirteenth day, with bread and cheese in our bags, we were headed south again on one of the main roads when I heard the rumbling of engines.

Jumping over the embankment filled with a foot of brackish water, we slid into the dense brush. I peered through the leaves as the ground began to vibrate and the noise grew to a roar.

A German military convoy crawled toward us at a snail's pace. Cars, horses, wagons, trucks and people clogged the road. The men looked grim, their uniforms filthy. They shuffled along on foot. The luckier ones were riding high on top of flatbeds. Many were injured.

I couldn't help but scan the men's faces inside the medical trucks. I saw their dulled eyes and bloody stumps. How still they lay. Some moaned. I felt relief when no one looked familiar. Maybe my father was long dead, lying frozen and forgotten in some mass grave.

"You think we should show ourselves?" Helmut said into my ear.

I shook my head as I stared longingly at the provisions trucks and wondered if these soldiers knew about Marburg. All it took was one zealous officer and we'd be turned in.

# DAY FIFTEEN

"I want to go home," Helmut said two days later as we hiked yet another forest path. "We're starving, and my shoes are falling apart."

"What if someone sees us?" I said, trying to ignore my own eagerness for a warm bed.

"We'll be careful."

"Just for a day, then?"

Helmut nodded, a grim smile on his face.

It took us two more days to reach our neighborhood. Everything seemed to be the same and I breathed a sigh of relief to see my house standing solid in the dark. I snuck through the basement door and tiptoed my way upstairs. Muffled voices drifted into the hall. I had to be absolutely sure nobody saw me. I tried the entrance door. It was locked.

"Who's there?" Siegfried asked from the other side.

"I'm back," I whispered. The door flew open. I slipped inside just as Mother ran from the kitchen.

"Günter!"

With a sigh I relaxed into her warmth.

"What're you doing here?" she said. "It's not over, is it?"

"No, *Mutter*. But we overheard some soldiers—the Americans are already in *Siegen*. The Army is retreating everywhere."

Mother shook her head. "You can't stay. If someone sees you…"

"I know." I'd never wanted anything more. "Have you heard…" From father and Hans I'd intended to say, but my voice didn't obey.

"Nothing, no letter." Mother avoided my eyes and hurried to the breadbox. "I'll fix you something to eat."

Like I'd done at the old man's farm, I closed my eyes as I ate the cornbread. Mother seemed thinner than two weeks ago and I wondered if I was eating her ration. Still chewing I walked to my room. My bed looked warm and inviting. I wanted to curl up and sleep forever.

Mother followed. "You better stay in the basement. I heard the SS just shot several people for picking up leaflets."

"What did the flyer say?" I asked, wandering back into the kitchen.

"That we should surrender when the Americans come." Mother sagged on the bench. "Hitler wants to kill us all first. Promise me to be careful. I'll get you an extra blanket."

When no footsteps or voices could be heard above, I quietly opened the entrance door and snuck downstairs. I was hungry again, but that couldn't be helped. I locked myself into the coal cellar and spread out on an old mattress we kept down here for bomb alarms.

I awoke from the rapping on the door.

"Better get up," Mother whispered. I unlocked and snuck upstairs. After the warmth of my bed, the kitchen felt like an icebox. "We're short on wood," Mother said as if she'd heard my thoughts.

It would've been easy for me to scrounge firewood, but I couldn't risk it. The SS often appeared out of nowhere, and many people had disappeared after being turned in by spying or opportunistic neighbors like the man who'd stolen our horse last December. With a sigh, I pulled on my coat and sat down to a piece of cornbread and peppermint tea. I left the next evening at dusk, picking up Helmut on the way.

The air had warmed, the beginnings of spring tinged bushes and trees with fresh green. We kept hiking, some paths familiar, but it was hard to tell anymore. Entire forests were disappearing, either bombed and burned or cut down for firewood.

# DAY TWENTY

I could never get used to the cold. No matter how fast we walked or how we wrapped ourselves in coat, hat and gloves, the wintry air crept into my bones. First, it sat on top, just a whiff as if somebody breathes on your wet skin. You shiver a bit, but get distracted and forget.

But the cold doesn't stop there. It is sneaky and mean as it knocks past the skin and climbs inside you. There it spreads with thousand tentacles until your insides freeze and your muscles stiffen and ache. Shivering is no longer an option, it's a must. You have no choice. That's when you get scared to fall asleep and die of hypothermia. When you jump up and windmill your arms to pump the slush in your blood.

Whenever I got this cold, I thought of home. I couldn't help myself. Mother's soups came to mind, the red-hot stovetop in the midst of winter, fed by the comfortable heat from the seasoned roof trusses we scavenged from bombsites. I'd thought it had been hard after the bombing, the 'Angriff' last November when Solingen burned down. I'd been angry about the additional work fixing the roof and our windows, having no running water or electricity.

Now I knew that even the little we'd retained, had been comfort. Mother and Siegfried had been there. I'd slept in a bed and sat at a table.

Out here in the hilly land I'd always loved and considered familiar, I was at a loss, a drifter at the whim of a madman.

Another thing I noticed was the quality of time. In misery,

time has a tendency to slow down. Every minute stretches, an hour feels like four and a day lengthens into a week. Your thoughts turn in circles, cloud your perception.

On day twenty we found a frozen bird, some kind of pigeon with grayish white feathers and clouded eyes.

"You think it's still good?" Helmut poked the rigid body with a stick.

I bent low to sniff. Nothing but earthiness hit my nose. The bird's body was intact. "Let's try a fire and see."

We were on a hillside overlooking a patch of evergreens so we headed into the woods to better hide the fire.

The bird was hard as an ice cube, so we laid it on a rock beside the flames. Luckily, there was little smoke because the evergreen trees had produced plenty of twigs, many even dry.

"Wonder what it tastes like," I mumbled as I turned the bird yet again. Its neck was soft now and lay at an angle.

"I'm going to gut it," Helmut said. "Used to help Father clean rabbits," he continued, his voice dreamy.

I watched as he positioned the bird on its back and slit it open from neck to belly. Innards burst from the cut. I swallowed and made myself busy feeding the fire.

"I think it's all right," Helmut said, rubbing his hands with pine needles. He'd cut off head and feet too.

Relieved, I quickly carved a stick to a point and skewered the bird, trying to ignore the thought of worms and maggots slithering inside.

"Wonder what it died from," Helmut said as we took turns holding the bird above the fire. The air reeked with the stench of burning and melting feathers.

"Old age?"

Helmut stared at me and then ever so slowly his expression grew into a smile. A giggle rose from my throat, so strange and yet, so good. Helmut followed and soon we were laughing so hard, my ribs ached and Helmut sputtered for breath.

The aroma of roasting meat made us stop. Our gazes turned to the pigeon as if we were hypnotized. I couldn't look away, my mouth flooded with saliva. I wanted to rip the thing off its skewer and sink my teeth in and it took all my self-control to remain sitting on the wooden stump.

"Come on, get done already." As usual, Helmut echoed my

feelings.

Oh, hunger, you nasty brother. Always present, always nagging. Didn't we have enough worries already? Yet, Russians and Americans, the SS and assorted fanatics paled when it came to an empty stomach. In a way, hunger was a mightier enemy than people. Like the cold, it was sneaky and quiet. Always present, always on your mind. Causing pain in places you didn't know you had. Hunger shoved aside logical thoughts, our prudence we so desperately needed. It would almost cost us our lives.

Helmut carefully cut the bird in two pieces and we feasted.

# DAY TWENTY-THREE

The light was fading and we still hadn't found a suitable place to sleep. Usually, we scoped out an area during daylight so we knew what to expect. But our vigilance was waning. I often daydreamed to escape the gnawing fury in my middle. At least it wasn't raining and the forest floor, soft with fir needles, buffered our steps. The pleasant sharp smell of sap lay in the air and I took deep breaths.

"Damn, I don't even see a hunting blind," Helmut said over his shoulder. He was a couple of steps ahead, his voice deeper than I remembered, though he was as skinny as ever.

"Or a barn."

"Let's hurry then—"

"Can't see more than five feet with this stupid undergrowth." Indeed, this part of the woods hadn't been cleared or picked clean and brush and blackberry bushes tore at our clothes. The terrain was leading downhill into a narrow valley. Somewhere ahead water gurgled.

Likely that meant no people. It meant safety, but it also meant nothing to eat.

We were climbing across a pile of mushy tree trunks when I heard a rumbling. "Wruff, wruff."

In the waning light it was hard to tell where the sound

had come from.

Helmut froze and turned to look at me. I shook my head. Puffs of white breath rose between us. My mind sped up. Was there a road ahead...snipers...the SS? I felt the blood rush through my neck. My hands were clammy, damp, neither hot nor cold. Looking at my friend kept me from running, kept the panic in my bones contained.

Above us fir boughs whispered, but the forest held its breath—the silence absolute.

"What *was* that?" Helmut whispered.

I shrugged. "Let's hurry before it gets totally dark."

We jumped off the log pile when all hell broke loose. High-pitched squeals mixed with deep grunts as a wild sow broke from between two trees not six feet away. In the twilight she was almost invisible, her gray coat shaggy, her small eyes on us.

"Run," Helmut cried, the panic in his voice almost as frightening as the angry sow.

*Where to*, I wanted to say, but it was too late. The sow rushed me with such power that I smashed to the ground. Wet leaves hit my face, followed by searing pain. My calf screamed and a moan filled my ears. I don't know if that's what scared the sow away or if Helmut's crazy shouts from the top of the log pile stopped her. He'd climbed back up and stood there like an apparition, waving a huge tree limb.

I wanted to laugh because he looked so funny but that's when the pain crawled up my thigh into my hip and down to my toes. *The sow bit me*...bit clear through my pants and socks. It hurt worse than when I tore my shin in the barbwire a few years ago.

Helmut's face appeared above me. He was pale, the fuzz above his lip damp.

"She's gone," he panted. "She had young. We scared her." I followed his gaze to my leg where a dark stain spread along my calf.

"Damn," I cried.

I sat up with effort and I leaned forward. I didn't

want to look, but my eyes were drawn to the darkening spot. Helmut gingerly lifted the seam of my pants. Even that slight movement sent me through the roof. Air rushed from my throat in a gasp.

Helmut kneeled closer. "Hold still," he said. I couldn't see the wound very well because the bite was on the right backside of my calf and it was growing seriously dark now. "We've got to get you to a doctor," he said quietly. I heard the concern in his voice. In a way it worried me more than his usual loud complaints. "You might need a shot of something…maybe stitches."

I grunted in response because the throbbing was growing stronger—even overpowering my hunger. A gurgle rose from my throat, sort of a mix between laughter and a sob.

"I guess I've got an excuse now," I said.

"What?" Helmut sounded exasperated.

"I mean, if they ask us why we didn't go to Marburg."

Helmut mumbled something and held out a hand. "Come on, I'll help you."

When I straightened, the pain expanded again. It was a live thing with a pulse like its own heart. Putting weight on the leg made the pain grow further. I thought of the soldier with the missing arm who we'd helped cut wood. Losing a limb had to be infinitely harder.

We stumbled forward, each step a challenge. It was getting even harder to see and my leg had a mind of its own. In front of us the gurgling grew louder.

The creek was tiny, no more than three feet. Ordinarily, I would've jumped across, but now I stepped smack in the middle, soaking my right shoe. Freezing cold joined the thumping in my leg.

When I stumbled, I felt Helmut's arm on my side. By the time we reached the top of the hill, it was dark. Ahead lay a narrow road, reflecting a bit of moonlight. We began walking. *Let them catch us*, I thought. *At least I'd be able to lie down.*

I didn't know how much time had passed, but at some point we saw lights ahead. Those were joined by other lights. Nothing bright like a city, more like a village.

Helmut helped me lean against the entry door of a modest home before he deftly stepped to the entrance. In the overhead light, the door shone bright green. I took it as a good sign.

I didn't hear much of the talk, my focus on the pain that was taking over my body.

A shadow appeared next to me, then another and I felt myself lifted.

"Let's put him in the spare room," a woman's voice said. "I'll go and get the doctor."

I didn't know if a minute or an hour passed, but at some point an older man bent over my leg. He asked for more light and a pillow before rolling me on my side and propping up my leg.

I wanted to scream then, felt my forehead grow damp, then wet. The wall in front of me was white with little specks of gray like the footprint of tiny feet, so I focused on that.

"I've got to wash it clean," the man said.

"Here, bite on that," the same woman said. A washcloth appeared in front of my face and I took it between my teeth.

The next moment I wished for my leg to disappear. A burning sensation drilled into me, expanded, until it knocked on my bones. I wanted to kick…kick away the pain, the scraping soreness. But somebody was holding me still. I couldn't see anymore because my eyes were filled with tears that slipped past my nose into the pillow.

Oh, how I had wished to sleep in a bed. Just not this bed. Not this way.

"Should be good now," the same voice said. "I'll sow it up."

Tugging and a slight squeaky sound traveled to my ears. My mind was all foggy, but I heard that sound as loud as the live band we used to listen to in town.

I must have drifted off because when I awoke grayish light trickled into the window. With a pang I remembered last night, the scary sound, the sow's attack.

My leg throbbed dully, but not nearly as bad. I was covered with a feather comforter though the room was very frigid, my face cold.

I carefully touched my leg. It was bare—they'd taken off my pants—except for a bandage around the calf. I wiggled my big toe. Not too bad. But when I tried to move my ankle, the pain woke with it.

I lay back with a groan.

"You awake?" Helmut's sleepy voice drifted up from the floor. Seconds later he was by my side, hair standing on end. "Doctor says it'll be an ugly scar, but you'll be all right."

Despite the pain I smiled.

# DAY TWENTY-SEVEN

We stayed two days with the kind woman before taking off again. She'd repaired my pants and shared her meager supplies, but we were worried about her neighbors. The doctor who turned out to be a retired veterinarian had visited twice to sniff the wound and change the bandage. I was supposed to remove the five stitches in six days.

Anymore, I was losing track. The first three weeks I'd counted every day, but the monotony of our journey was softening my brain.

"It's been four weeks," Helmut said as if he'd heard me. Like some old married couple, he often said what I was thinking and vice versa. We were hiding inside an abandoned barn, its walls nearly collapsed around us. "What do you think Rolf is doing right now?"

"Wonder." I inspected my fingernails. They reminded me of the chimneysweeper who was always covered in soot and came by the house twice a year to remove coal dust. It had been in another century.

"I think we made a mistake," Helmut said, avoiding my eyes. "I mean, not going down there."

"Don't know." I imagined my classmates exploding with shouts and applause as Rolf Schlüter, his chest full of medals, marched into class. "I hate not getting any news," I managed.

"What if the war continues another year?"

I grimaced and jumped to my feet, the sudden move

making me wince. "I don't know." I was so tired. Tired of Helmut voicing the same questions and doubts I had myself and couldn't answer. Tired of being hungry and most of all, tired of being afraid. "Why don't you send a letter to Hitler and ask him what he plans?" I sneered. The anger was choking me like the insides of the bunker.

"I just mean I can't go on like this. My legs ache all the time." Helmut's voice had turned to a quiver.

"We'll have to." I punched the rough wood of the barn with my fist, welcoming the immediate pain. "How many times can you be lost? It's too late to show up in Marburg, even with the new scar."

"It's all your fault," Helmut said heatedly. He began to pace back and forth in the empty barn, his cheeks smoldering. "We should've gone down there. I shouldn't have listened to you." He threw up his arms and abruptly stopped in front of me. "You said the war would be over soon. But it's not. What if Hitler wins?"

"He won't."

"How do you know?"

"You heard what the soldiers said. You *saw* them—all torn up…retreating."

"Men say lots of things. People tried to kill him over and over. He always survived. Maybe he *is* invincible."

"He's like any other man, except insane."

"Why don't you admit that you were wrong?"

I shrugged. Maybe I was, but judging by Helmut's fury and balled fists, I wasn't about to admit it.

"Should have and would have," I scoffed instead.

Helmut sagged onto a pile of moldy straw. "You might as well have pulled the trigger. It's only a matter of time before the SS finds us. Or the Gestapo or one of their spies—"

"Shut up! Just shut up," I yelled. "I'm tired of your complaining. Why don't you go back and turn yourself in?"

I didn't want to admit that I felt just the same. My own legs were killing me, the sow's bite a dull throb. My stomach cramped most of the time and I felt surrounded by permanent darkness.

Helmut didn't leave, but after that we no longer talked. We took cues from each other, stopped to pee or take a break. I found myself listening to his breathing and his sighs, the way he cleared his throat. I wanted to say something, but the invisible wall between us held like reinforced concrete. We never looked at each other and we never spoke.

And with every day we got more exhausted until our gait resembled that of old men shuffling and dragging across the woods. We rested more, but the cold weather wasn't finished and we soon had to move again. A few times we risked a fire, the damp wood smoldering and giving off little heat. I worried about the smoke being seen.

More and more convoys clogged the roads. Plain soldiers snaked along in unending streams. I wasn't as afraid of them now because I knew they had little to do with the SS and Gestapo.

"Go home, boys," they whispered when we watched from the side of the street. "We have no ammunition left. The Americans are close."

*How close*, I wanted to shout. *How much longer?* All I did was nod, afraid to get into a discussion about our wanderings, afraid of looking at Helmut's face. We saw women pushing wheelbarrows with bedding, coffee grinders, pots and assorted suitcases, worn grandfathers with packs and children…small ones with thumbs in their mouths, some school age like my brother Siegfried. Everyone looked hungry and frightened.

# DAY THIRTY-FIVE

At last, we got brave enough to hitch a ride on one of the military trucks of a German convoy. Well, that is, I moved out into the line, hoping that Helmut would follow.

"Hop on up, boys," said one of the soldiers walking past. He smiled grimly through the muck on his face, his uniform jacket splattered with dried dirt.

So we scrambled onto one of the trucks, feet dangling over the edge.

"Did you see the truck behind us?" I shouted over the engine noise, somehow emboldened by our ride.

"No, why?" Helmut yelled back, his attention on one of the soldiers plopping down by the side of the road. The man's boots were torn and he was in the process of taking one off. The sock underneath was dotted with holes.

"They're loaded with food, you know, military bread."

"*Kommissbrot?*"

"We should ask for some." Without waiting for an answer, I jumped off the platform, immediately regretting it as a dull ache shot up my right calf. After passing two vehicles, I noticed a soldier marching alongside with his hands on a rifle. That had to be it. Sure enough, the provisions truck was stacked to its tarped ceiling with dark square loaves like shoe cartons.

"You think you could spare some bread?" I asked, thinking that it felt good to hear Helmut's voice.

The soldier, not much older than I, shot me an appraising

look. "Two loaves. We aren't going to slow down for you."

I glanced at the tall truck and the broad tires ready to squash me. I'd wait. "No problem, thanks." Then I yelled over at Helmut, "We can get some, but I'll have to wait to climb up till they stop or slow down enough."

He made a face and kept silent. Stubborn idiot.

When the road turned steep, the caravan decelerated to a crawl. The guard winked as I took hold of the back ramp and pulled myself up. I carefully selected two loaves and stuffed them in my shirt, making sure not to upset the load. Though the *Kommissbrot* was dry and hard, the whole rye, wheat and molasses would fill our stomachs like a real meal. I wondered if the rumors were true that they contained sawdust.

A shout made me look up. Like in a movie, the soldiers a few hundred yards back were jumping into ditches and running for the trees.

That's when I grew aware of a buzzing sound, growing rapidly louder as if someone had unleashed a giant nest of hornets. Gray specks appeared in the sky. They grew larger quickly—a squadron of low-flying enemy planes. Before I had time to act, machine gun fire exploded and the back of the convoy dissolved into a cloud of dust.

Terror crept up my legs. The shooting sensation of adrenalin hit my gut like a fist. I was in the open, ten feet above the road, a perfect target. There was no time to climb down and find Helmut on the other truck.

I jumped...flew...

Rat-a-tat-tat-tat...The ground rushed up to me. I rolled into the ditch as the sky darkened above me. Bullets shredded the bread truck, pierced tarps and metal with ease. I covered my head and lay still. My right calf throbbed—the noise was deafening. All I could do was lie there and wait and hope that none of the bullets or shrapnel found me.

When the blasts subsided, I sat up, noticing with relief that I was unhurt. Many others hadn't been so lucky. The sounds of human suffering drilled into my brain—men moaning and crying. My first impulse was to run. Run as far as my legs would carry me.

That's when I remembered Helmut, and cold panic seized me. What if Helmut had been shot? Unable to control my shaking hands, I scanned the road. Soldiers lay strewn between broken-down trucks like throwaway dolls. Most lay still.

I recognized the friendly guard from the bread truck a few feet away. He was on his back, eyes wide open, staring into the sky. His helmet had flown off, and the top of his skull was gone, reddish gray oozing onto the pavement.

Another man lay on his side near the ditch crying softly, "Help me." The front of his army coat had blown to shreds, his intestines visible. I tried to look away, but the man stared straight at me. Since I was still in the ditch we were at eye level.

The man had blond hair, shaven around the ears, his eyebrows brownish caterpillars that didn't match the reddish tinge of stubble on his chin. Blood gurgled from his mouth, and he sputtered as if he were under water. At last, he stopped moving, his gaze frozen.

I climbed out of the ditch. I had to find Helmut. In my confusion, I couldn't remember where I'd left him. My heart raced worse than when I'd run sprints in school. I hurried along the road, turned this way and that. I recognized the truck we'd been on, now broken down, shot to pieces. The wooden bed had splintered, its tires flat. Helmut wasn't there.

"Helmut?" I cried, voice high in my throat.

Men were running and shouting orders, checking for wounded and dead. I dashed around the broken-down truck. I checked the ditch. No Helmut.

With every step I grew more convinced that Helmut was dead and that I was alone, an island among the frantic activity around me. Until I couldn't walk any farther. I stood amidst the chaos, my mind blank, my body paralyzed.

"Günter?" Helmut's voice drifted through the fog. "Over here."

I turned on my heels, watching uncomprehendingly as Helmut rushed up to me. Mud stuck to his right cheek and temple, but he looked whole.

"I went to look for you," Helmut panted, his eyes huge in his face.

I searched for my voice. "I couldn't find you," I croaked. "I thought you were…"

Helmut patted me on the back, a grim smile on his lips. It was the first I'd seen since the pigeon roast. "I'm all right."

I grinned back, then glanced at the sky. "Let's go. They

may return."

We melted into the woods, the bread securely tucked in our jackets. During the night, I dreamed about the man with the reddish stubble. In my dream, the soldier sat up, pulling feet of intestines out of his belly. He laughed crazily as he kept piling them on the ground.

I awoke, my face sweaty and cold. I looked to my side where Helmut slept under a blanket. Only a few strands of sandy hair were visible. For a moment I felt intensely thankful that my friend was safe. I wanted to reach over and touch his shoulder, tell him that no matter what we'd stick together. It was the only thing that mattered, the only thing Hitler would not take away.

I sat up and broke off a piece of bread. It tasted metallic, as if it were tainted with blood.

# DAY FORTY

Nearly six weeks into our journey and after finding nothing but rotten potatoes in a deserted field, we reached a small village about sixty kilometers from home. A pub was the only official building. No matter how small a village, every place had at least one tavern.

Having no industry and being tucked into the hills, it seemed the war had passed this town by, at least as far as we could see. Houses and sheds were intact. Even the church steeple with its bronze bell, white stucco walls and a modest stained-glass window was unharmed. Several military trucks and jeeps parked a couple of hundred yards down the narrow street.

"You think they'll give us something to eat?" Helmut asked, sounding doubtful as we stared at the whitewashed walls of the *Gasthof Zum Löwen*. Lights shone from the inside, coloring the windows in a warm glow. The delicious aroma of roasted meat drifted across.

I tasted bile, and my insides churned. We hadn't eaten since yesterday, a handful of shriveled onions from last year. Risking a fire, we'd thrown our find into the wood coals and gulped them down half raw.

"Wait here, I'll go."

I stepped into the street. Nobody was around, though I suspected the trucks were well protected. Trying to keep up my resolve, I slipped into the pub.

With the low ceiling and darkly paneled walls, it felt as suffocating as a bunker. Thick smoke hung in the air. After the brightness of the evening sun, I squinted in the gloom.

A fat man in a black shirt and stained blue apron stood behind the counter, wiping up beer spills. The smell of something sour mixed with stale alcohol filled the air. I wondered how the man could serve food and liquor while nobody else had anything left.

Afraid to lose my confidence, I deftly stepped to the counter. Too late did I notice the military jackets.

I would've recognized the emblems anywhere: a jagged double S clearly visible on collars, armbands and hats: SS officers.

Three men occupied stools to the side of the bar, smoking and talking loudly, a selection of empty glasses in front of them. I silently swore as I glanced back at the entrance, my hunger forgotten.

To my horror, the room fell silent.

"What can I get you?" the barman said, his deep-set eyes black raisins within folds of doughy skin.

I licked my lips, scolding myself for being sloppy. Why hadn't I peeked through the windows first? Now it was too late. I stood smack into the middle of a nightmare.

If I screwed up now, we'd be done for. I *had* to appear confident.

"My friend and I are looking for a small meal," I said, forcing air through my lungs. "We don't have money, but we can work."

"Another beggar." The barkeeper addressed the officers with a mock grin.

Ignoring the men in the corner, I shook my head. "We'll work for what we get."

"Let's hear him out," one of the officers said.

"What can you do?" The barkeeper asked with a detached voice.

"Chores," I stammered, "like dishes, cut wood, or we can repair stuff. I'm good at fixing things." I looked around the room in search of an obvious item in need of maintenance. The silence grew. I could feel the officers' eyes burning into me.

One of the men leaned forward. "What about fixing our country?"

The officer next to him chuckled. "It'll take more than hammer and nails."

I noticed that the third man hadn't joined the laughter. He looked irritated, his eyes gleaming as coldly as distant stars. Unsure what to do and afraid they'd ask more questions, I stumbled on, "We can work first and you can give us food afterward, as payment."

Why didn't I just shut up and leave? The SS and their obvious arrogance meant nothing but trouble or worse. As I stood rooted to the middle of the pub room, the officers began to whisper.

"Oh, come on, barkeep. Give the boy a break." One of the officers came over.

I did a double take. The guy looked like an older Birdsnest, the boy who'd tormented me in the Hitler Youth a thousand years ago. He had the same blond hair, shaved along the sides, leaving a tuft of curls on top. I couldn't be sure. Five years had passed, but for a moment I worried if Birdsnest would recognize me.

"Here, I'll pay for his dinner." The man tossed down twenty *Reichsmark*, something I hadn't seen in a while. The bartender mumbled but took the money. "Better get your comrade, then. Looks like you have a new friend."

"I'll be right back." Now was my chance to disappear. Fast. I turned on my heels and sprinted off, colliding with Helmut outside the front door. Trying to control my panic, I frantically blinked at Helmut, furious with myself for neglecting to set up a distress signal.

"How did it go?" Helmut asked innocently. "I am soooo hungry, I could eat a house."

"I don't—"

"Hello there," someone said behind me.

I flinched. *Breathe.* Luckily I had my back turned. Helmut's eyes widened as the blond SS-man in the immaculate uniform, the high black boots waxed to a perfect shine, stepped into the street.

"What're you waiting for? Your food is ready."

I managed a nod, my throat too tight to speak. *Run away now*, my gut urged. *Run and you'll be shot*, my mind argued. We had to play along. Either way we were dead.

The barkeep appeared as soon as we sat down in one of the booths by the window, his huge stomach hidden behind a white porcelain bowl and plates. "Enjoy."

I swallowed and reached for the ladle. The dark venison

stew smelled heavenly. I wanted nothing more than to eat, yet my belly churned with fear. Helmut looked almost green. We had to talk normally or raise suspicion. I managed a weak nod and filled my plate.

To my relief the barman reappeared, shielding us from the SS-men. "Bread and beer, courtesy of your new friends."

I eyed the glass before nodding in the general direction of the counter. I wanted to be drunk and forget everything. But alcohol made you careless.

"May I have some water, please?" I asked, my voice foreign in my ears.

I knew the officers were watching us, so I grabbed the fork and slowly began to chew. The rich sauce exploded in my mouth, my taste buds doing overtime. The bread was warm and the crust thick and fragrant. I forgot the men and our situation, my stomach demanding to be heard.

Amazing how you could still eat when your head was already in a noose.

I watched Helmut who was chewing hard, his eyes glazed. We kept eating until the last of the stew had disappeared and the breadbasket was empty. I leaned back and belched. My stomach roiled with a mix of cold fear and too much food. Why hadn't I thought of an excuse to leave? I was just thinking of what to say to Helmut when Birdsnest materialized at the table.

"*Obersturmführer* Kummel, may I sit?"

It *was* Birdsnest. I cleared my throat, hoping that my voice didn't wobble. "Nice to meet you."

"Thanks for dinner," Helmut offered, his gaze hanging on the officer a moment too long. Helmut had made the same connection.

"Where are you boys headed?" Birdsnest asked. I stared at Helmut, trying to decide what to say. Helmut's cheeks were as pale as the tablecloth.

*I've got to say something.* "We're going to Marburg. Trying to get there on foot."

"Show me your orders!" Birdsnest held out his hand. I scrambled to find my papers. What if the officer asked where we were from? How could we be north of where we'd started when Marburg was quite a bit south?

Instead of studying our papers, Birdsnest jumped up. "Did

you hear that?" he asked, addressing the officers at the bar. "These two are going to Marburg."

"You don't say." Another officer approached our table. "Didn't they give the order to Marburg weeks ago?" He scratched his head.

I froze. This time it wouldn't be pushups—this time we'd be lined up outside and shot. To my surprise, I still breathed, my clammy palms under the table, my feet cold, toes rubbing against the leather. Why didn't I just fall over and lose consciousness? Get it over with?

"…is your lucky day," the officer was just saying.

"What?" I croaked, coming out of a daze.

Birdsnest jumped in eagerly, "We're heading to Frankfurt. You can hop in the back of our truck and," Birdsnest paused, "Harald, you don't suppose we can take a little side trip to drop off these fine young soldiers?" The third officer, who scrutinized us without speaking, stood up.

"I'm sure."

Birdsnest, now with a proud note said, "You see, you'll get to fight very soon. We need every man."

I choked and hurried to cough. Looking up from my plate, Harald's arctic eyes met mine. Forcing my mouth into a smile, I glanced at Helmut whose upper lip trembled.

"Harald, isn't that great?" Birdsnest chuckled. But Harald didn't speak—he kept staring at me.

"That's wonderful," I blurted. "When are you going? We're pretty tired. We walked all day."

The second officer nodded toward the ceiling. "We sleep upstairs. Meet us here at 05:30."

Birdsnest stood up, snapped his right arm into the air, "*Heil Hitler!*" The other officers followed suit and we raised our arms.

"A little more enthusiasm, perhaps?" Harald wandered over, his voice high, almost girlish.

"Ah, leave them alone." Birdsnest slapped his comrade on the back. "They'll learn soon enough. A few weeks of training and they'll be ready to take on the Russians."

Harald nodded but kept staring as if he wanted to decide whether to shoot or cut us into pieces.

I straightened, thankful my legs were holding up. "We

better rest so we'll be ready for the trip."

"You can sleep over there." The barkeeper pointed to a side room with tables and benches. "It's hard but I guess you're used to that."

"We'd be happy to sleep in your shed," I suggested. "We don't want to take up any space." I hoped we might escape if we were outside the building. Especially since it was getting dark.

"No need boys." The bartender smiled. "I'll make room for the young soldiers of our fatherland."

"Thanks," I managed. I had to buy time. We couldn't run out. That would surely raise suspicion. This fellow Harald looked as if he'd enjoy shooting us on the spot.

"We better find the outhouse. Do you have water outside?"

The barkeep pointed to the back door. "Through there, take a right. The outhouse is straight back. There's a faucet next to the house."

"Come on, Helmut." I headed to the backdoor, hoping to look enthusiastic. To my horror, the barman followed and ambled past us.

"Right over there is the latrine. And here's the water."

Without another word, I entered the outhouse. Sweat dripped underneath my shirt. *Breathe.* The stench was overpowering. I needed time to think, but there was no quiet spot. It'd be suspicious if we stayed out too long. My head was numb. The more I tried to concentrate, the more panicky I felt.

I stepped outside, slamming the door shut. Helmut was leaning against the house, his eyes wide with panic.

"Now what?" he whispered, his voice shaking with anger. "Why did I listen to you? They'll find out as soon as we get to Marburg. Maybe even earlier…"

I just shook my head, my eyes imploring Helmut to be quiet. Somewhere above us a window opened. Our worst nightmare was coming true.

We'd be taken to Marburg and then we'd be executed. I thought of Mother, imagined her pacing the silent apartment, stopping in front of the empty beds. I opened the faucet to cool my burning face. The water was freezing but I didn't feel it. My gamble had failed. Tomorrow we'd die.

To my relief the officers had gone upstairs when we

reentered the pub.

"I'll bolt the doors." The barkeep didn't wait for an answer and the room grew dark. We were locked in.

Heat and cold took turns on my skin. My throat tightened, the feeling of an invisible hand choking the air out of me. I was back in the bunker…in…out…in…out.

"Listen," I whispered, concentrating on every breath, "we have to disappear before morning. If they take us down there, it's over."

Helmut leaned closer. "If they catch us fleeing, we'll be dead, too."

"We'll leave between two and three. That should give us enough time to safely disappear."

"But the doors are locked. How will we get out?"

"Through the windows."

"But where are we going? What if they follow us? Or somebody is outside watching? They probably have guards." Helmut's whispers grew louder. "It's all your fault."

"Shhh!" I hissed. "We'll go south." I was mad at Helmut for talking and saying the things I'd been thinking. Most of all I was mad at myself for letting my guard down, for allowing my hunger to lead us into danger.

"They won't expect that," I said. "We'll keep away from the roads. One of us has to stay awake. We'll take turns. There's a clock in the main bar. You take the first watch. Wake me in two hours. It's nine now. Do *not* fall asleep."

Despite my sluggish mind and the unaccustomed beer I'd been too weak to refuse, I had trouble relaxing. I worried about Helmut falling asleep or worse, telling the officers. What if he turned me in to save his own neck? Impossible. We'd been friends as long as I remembered. The bench creaked under Helmut's weight. I nodded off.

I dreamed my father walked into the bar. He was smiling and ordering rounds of beer for the SS-men. A hole gaped where his stomach had been. He was laughing as he tipped his drink, beer pouring from his middle. I screamed and awoke.

The first thing I noticed was that I was freezing and the second that I couldn't see Helmut in the darkness.

"What time is it?" I whispered.

Nothing. What if he's gone to tell the officers, the voice in my head commented.

"Helmut?" Relief spread as I detected even breathing nearby. Remembering the clock, I carefully tiptoed into the main bar.

With one hand outstretched I felt my way to the counter. The clock was somewhere on the wall. I walked along the bar, running my hands across the top where I'd seen matches yesterday. Even in the dark I could tell that my hands shook. My fingers caught on the matchbox and the phosphor exploded into flame.

Raising the light toward the clock, I blinked. It was four-fifteen. We'd slept more than seven hours.

Panic gripped me. Fingertips burning I dropped the match. It turned dark as my mind began to race. Any minute the men would be up. I hurried back, shoving Helmut in the shoulder.

"Wake up."

Helmut yawned. "I fell asleep."

I wanted to strangle him. "It's really late."

Helmut grumbled. "What time is it?"

"Hurry," I whispered, "from now on not a word. We'll head straight through the backyard."

"Fine," said Helmut, making the bench creak all over again.

Groping in the dark, I found the window latch and pushed. I'd thought about our escape route last night. With the doors locked, windows were our only chance.

The window didn't budge.

What if the frames had been nailed shut? I hadn't thought of that. We'd be locked in.

Again, I lifted the handle. Something screeched, wood scraping against wood. I pushed harder.

The window reluctantly gave and I held my breath to listen. Any sound would travel. What if the SS had men stationed around the inn? Surely there were guards somewhere close. My breath rattled in the silence. The air outside was windless and absolutely still while my heart pounded in my head so loud that I was sure they heard me upstairs.

I lifted one leg across the sill. Carefully shifting my weight, my foot hit the ground outside. Something crunched and I froze. Ever so slowly I added more pressure. Something beneath my foot broke like a firecracker. New panic rose in my throat. *Run.* I pulled the other leg out quickly and threw myself into the darkness, hoping to land on something soft. Watery grass blades hit my face.

"Wait." I scrambled to my knees and rummaged across the ground. I couldn't see Helmut, but heard his movement in the window. Something jagged cut my hand, a piece of glass or shard, some forgotten flowerpot. I managed to pull away my fingers just as Helmut's foot hit the ground. Again I listened.

All I heard was Helmut's labored breath and my own heart pounding in my neck.

I looked up where I knew the second floor windows to be. It was impossible to tell if any stood open. If someone upstairs couldn't sleep and stood by the window, he would certainly hear us. That grim officer, Harald, was creepy, kind of sinister. I had no doubt Harald would execute us.

I shivered.

The air smelled damp and thick with wetness. It clung to my skin, penetrated my coat, and turned my fingers stiff. Not daring to speak, I stretched one arm to the side, touching Helmut's shoulder. The other hand reached straight ahead. I tried recalling the landscape behind the garden, vaguely remembering trees and bushes. Why hadn't I paid better attention?

A dog barked in the distance, a detached sound, ghostly, impossible to tell how far away. I heard Helmut suck in air, his fear palpable in the darkness. *You've got to be strong.* I carried on, one step…another. It was impossible to tell where we were going. If we wandered off course, we might run straight into a guard or one of the military trucks. I willed my ears, all my senses to lead us.

There was no room for error. Not now. I couldn't let it happen. My thighs wanted to cramp, weak and shaky at the same time. Still, I placed my feet carefully, moved in painful slowness.

A terrible stink reached my nose as my fingers touched something rough. The outhouse. We'd only made it a few yards.

A door slammed behind us and my knees gave. I dragged Helmut with me. A light danced toward us. Somebody shuffled across the lawn. Any second we'd be seen.

We crept around the outhouse away from the light. A loud yawn reverberated, a door squeaked, followed by the unmistaken sound of things dropping below. I tried holding my breath to avoid smelling the stench. I wondered if it was the barkeep.

The dewy grass poked my skin like icy fingers and I began

to shiver. The barkeep would find us gone and tell the SS-men. Why hadn't we closed the window to make it less obvious? I was too stupid.

I hardly noticed when the door slammed and the man moved away. He noisily scratched his body as his shadow dissolved into blackness.

Helmut punched my shoulder. "Let's go."

We straightened and wordlessly, one shaky arm outstretched, stumbled forward. It was like walking into a void, a black hole with nothing to guide us, every step a new risk. Brush slapped my face and I closed my eyes. It was just as well. Every minute seemed like an hour, every step a mile. My knees were soft with dread.

Without warning, my hand struck something firm—bark. We went around, stumbling across roots and stones. Another tree rose up. And another. What if we were going in circles?

"Can we rest for a minute?" Helmut whispered.

"Only a minute." I fell to the ground, not caring about the spongy wetness.

"How long do you think since we left?"

"We haven't gone far enough." I envisioned the nasty officer barking orders, saw dogs sniffing, teeth bared and then—

"I wish it were light," Helmut said. "I hope we're heading in the right direction."

"We better go."

After a few feet we ran into another tree. Limbs rustled above, a whisper—it had to be a forest.

Another dog barked. It seemed farther away. We kept walking, last night's dinner a faint memory.

Helmut abruptly stopped and cried, "Ouch, my hand," just as I felt something sharp digging into my waist.

"Barbed wire." I cursed the darkness, blindly feeling for more wires. There were three, the lowest a foot above ground.

"Where do you think this is going?" Helmut asked. "Maybe we should walk around."

"Better go straight," I said, imagining a mad bull charging us on the other side. Cows were a thing of the past. If there were any, the farmers hid them well. "I want to go as far as possible from the inn."

"Wonder how far we've come," Helmut said again.

*He always says the things I'm thinking. We've been together too long.* But then I remembered the bombers and how I'd thought I'd lost Helmut. And I knew then that I'd rather stick with Helmut until I couldn't walk another step than to spend one hour alone. "Slide across the ground. I'll hold up the wire," I said aloud.

Helmut dropped to his knees and scooted low. "Now you."

The grass was an icy bath as the wire scraped across my back. The trees had ended which felt like walking in space. We had no reference, no direction. Only the ground sloped lower.

"Let's wait here until dawn," I finally said.

The grass was short with tough blades, the ground squishy and I soon began to shiver. Faintly in the distance we heard sounds.

"You think they're looking for us?" Helmut asked.

"Don't know. You'd think they have better things to do than chase a couple of boys."

"Hope so."

When dawn broke, we found ourselves on a former pasture. Behind us, the land rose toward the trees. Ahead, it fell into a long valley, a patch of woods to our left.

"Let's hide in the forest," I said. Continuing toward the trees, I fought the urge of looking over my shoulder.

We collapsed in the gloom of a pine stand. Needles covered the ground, and the air was filled with the sharp aroma of pine tar. How I longed for a fire. We were drenched with a mixture of sweat and dew, the skin on our hands hard and dry, fingers bony, knuckles scraped bloody.

I wanted to be home, take a hot bath and go to bed with a warm comforter and clean sheets. I thought of the other beds, my father's and my brother's which had been empty much longer.

Lately, I'd been having a hard time remembering my father's face. Everything was turning blurry, even the memories of how life had been before the war. I thought of Mother standing in the kitchen, looking at Siegfried, the last child, the last person at home and I longed for her embrace, her smile or even her scolding look when I'd forgotten to do a chore.

# DAY FORTY-SEVEN

Helmut sat up from his makeshift bed underneath a hazelnut bush. It was too early to carry fruit, but the fresh green was thick.

"I want to visit home. I could really use a bed for a day or two."

I jumped up. "That's the best idea you've had all day."

Seven weeks had passed since we'd left for the woods. It seemed a lifetime ago. Now that I thought about it, I couldn't stand living this way another second—even if it meant being home for a few hours.

We hiked cross-country until I recognized the hills of the *Wupper* valley.

"Did you see that?" Helmut pointed at a couple of houses in the tiny village of *Wupperhof.* "They have white sheets hanging out the window. You think somebody died?"

"Maybe." I thought of the city bombing last November when white sheets had signaled dead bodies ready for pickup.

Pushing the thought of swirling flies and decomposition from my mind, I concentrated on the happy face Mother would have when she saw me. I couldn't wait to see her.

"I don't know how much longer I can do this," Helmut sighed.

"It should be over soon. Remember what the soldiers said." How often had I repeated these words? Rolf Schlüter returned to my memory, showing off his medals in class, sneering and pointing his pistol at me. *Deserter,* he said. *Arrest him.*

I walked faster. Anything was better than to think about the consequences of my actions. I was blind to the fact that spring had finally arrived. Though the leaves from last winter rustled underfoot, the trees were bright green, bathing us in shadows.

"There's another sheet," Helmut said, panting and holding his sides. "Do you think they have some kind of disease? The house isn't bombed."

"I can't imagine what it would be."

"What about typhus—you get it from bad water."

"Maybe they poisoned the wells or the reservoir." I kept walking. "If the Americans and Russians are close..."

"What're we going to drink?"

"We'll have to get water from a stream and boil it." What if Mother had gotten sick and died? I hadn't been home in weeks. Lots of things could happen, sometimes within an hour or a split second. I quickened my pace.

"Slow down!" Helmut massaged his ribs, panting. "I'm tired."

But I couldn't stop, even if my legs burned and my throat had turned to sandpaper. I had to get home. Now. Never mind it was daytime. That we were in plain sight.

By the time we arrived in the neighborhood, my lungs ached, and I was wheezing.

"Let's meet again tomorrow night. I'll pick you up after dark." I didn't wait for Helmut's answer and sprinted up the street. On *Weinsbergtalstraße* I slowed down—then sighed. The apartment houses still stood.

But the street seemed strangely deserted, and I noticed more white sheets. There was my house. Finally. I scanned the windows of my family's apartment. Nothing. But wait. There was a sheet on the side. I hadn't noticed it at first, but something white hung on the side of the building, my parents' bedroom.

Mother had died.

Dread crept up my spine like icy fingers, urging me to sprint the last bit. The apartment door was locked and I retrieved the spare key from under the mat, something Mother and I had agreed upon when I left.

"*Mutter?*"

Nothing. As my eyes adjusted to the gloom I ran, checking every room—the apartment was empty. They'd taken Mother away.

Siegfried was probably dead, too.

I sat down heavily, a deep sob building in my chest. Pain spread through me like acid and burned a hole where my heart had been. I'd wait here till the SS picked me up or a bomb fell on me. I glanced around the clean and orderly room, my father's favorite leather chair. It'd been empty for five years. Now I was truly alone.

Tears streamed unchecked. Time stood still.

Images of my family danced in my head: eating a meal, Mother baking a pie, my father repairing an outlet, Siegfried galloping around the house, pretending to be a horse, Hans lying on his bed reading a book. They kept circling, drawing me in, a swirl spinning faster and faster, pulling me down and away. The air turned black and thick as molasses—too hard to breathe.

Would my lungs simply stop? After my experience in the bunker when I had experienced claustrophobia for the first time, I'd often thought about choking to death. It made you want to jump out of your body for fear of drowning.

"Günter?" Mother plunked down her water buckets and rushed to my side.

I looked up, taking in Mother's slight figure, the patched coat and the scarf wrapped around her head. Was I dreaming? Only one way to find out. I jumped up and threw myself into Mother's arms.

"Am I glad to see you," I choked.

"Are you all right?" Mother held me tightly. "What happened?"

"I thought you… the sheets in the window."

"Oh you thought…" Mother shook her head. "This time it's not a sign of dead people. You didn't hear?"

I stared. What was she talking about?

"It's over. The Americans are in town. Solingen has surrendered. That's why we have the sheets out." Mother touched my cheek.

"The war is over."

The End

# EPILOGUE

I watched Mother disappear into the kitchen, yet all I could see was Helmut's dirt-smeared face, the way he'd looked after the bombers almost got us on the road.

*It's over. Over.*

No more hiding. No more running through the woods, afraid of meeting the wrong men. After six years, Hitler's foul veil had been lifted. Never again would I need to hide in the basement or sneak out after dark. Helmut and I could walk the street without that creepy feeling somebody was watching.

"Better come and eat." Mother's voice drifted into my consciousness. "Afterwards, I could use some help with firewood."

As I got up to join my family, a chuckle burst from my throat.

I was finally free.

Of course, that moment didn't last. Happiness is but a fleeting emotion. Like a blast of hot air in a cold room, it tends to vanish. As postwar Germany began, it ushered in new pressing questions. How would we survive in the rubble when there was no food, no work and no money? But most of all, what had happened to Father and Hans?

# AUTHOR NOTE

The *Volkssturm* or people's storm was Hitler's last propaganda command, not organized by the German military but the NSDAP, the Nazi party. All able-bodied men between 16 and 60 were classified into four groups from most usable to least usable. My father, Günter, born in December 1928, had just turned 16 and was in classification III. Military training was supposed to take place within the Hitler Youth (HJ) by the end of March 1945. At this point in the war, allied troops had been on German ground for months, German soldiers on the retreat. Weapons and equipment were almost impossible to find. It is reported that more than 1.3 million guns were needed, but only 18,000 available. Machine guns were even more rare: 75,000 were needed and 180 available. Originally, the *Volkssturm* was supposed to defend the home front. In the case of my father, the boys were ordered to find their way about 200 km south to Marburg. I assume this was done in an attempt to stop the advancing U.S. Armies who were already in *Siegen*, less than sixty miles from Marburg. One can only imagine what happened when these youngsters were confronted with fully equipped and trained U.S. troops. Did they even have guns or did they attempt to stop tanks with their bare hands?

70% of these boys who'd grown up during the Nazi reign, volunteered. How many boys and men served during the *Volkssturm* is unknown. Their effect was negligible. They could not even protect single homes, not to mention a professional army.

To some readers it may appear that this act of defiance, of not answering conscription is nothing special. My father didn't shoot SS-men nor did he plan an assassination on Hitler. He was neither a killer nor was he in the resistance. But he did one important thing many much older and mature people neglect to do. He thought for himself. Then he took a gamble and followed through on his conviction. The way I see it, this was extremely difficult, considering how much pressure was put on the people to follow orders. In a dictatorship refusing to follow orders means certain punishment. In my father's case, it would've meant certain death because even in the spring of 1945, cells of fanatical SS-men remained and many innocent people were shot.

None of Günter's classmates were ever heard of or seen again.

# TIMELINE

March 5, 1945
In the desperate last wave of the *Volkssturm,* Hitler orders all boys, born 1928 and 1929 to defend the 'fatherland.'

April 16/17, 1945
American troops arrive in Solingen. Its citizens surrender without a fight.

April 21, 1945
Battle of Berlin, 2.5 million Red Army soldiers surround the city, fighting one million German soldiers. The last fanatics, SS, Hitler youth create stand-up desertion tribunals, shooting surrendering German citizens on the spot.

April 30, 1945
Hitler commits suicide.

May 2-8, 1945
The German government surrenders.

# CHARACTERS

## GÜNTER 1928-

Günter became a master dye maker and ran his own company for seven years. In 1970, he joined Hugo Pott, a world-renowned silverware company and became a lead designer. His unique expertise, a combination of artistry and technical knowledge, made him a sought-after employee all his life. He had two daughters (one is the author) with his wife, Helga, and retired at age 70. Always figuring he'd be the first to die, he was devastated when Helga fell ill. After her death, he struggled to find meaning in his life, but the grit that accompanied him all his life saved him. He remains independent, still lives in the same house and is active with his nature ponds and garden.

# HELMUT 1928-1992

Helmut became a typesetter and had two children with his wife Helga. A heavy smoker all his life, he contracted lung cancer and passed away in 1992. Günter and Helmut remained casual friends all their lives.

# HELMUT AND GÜNTER, 1949

# ABOUT THE AUTHOR

 Annette Oppenlander is an award-winning writer, literary coach and educator. As a bestselling historical novelist, Oppenlander is known for her authentic characters and stories based on true events, coming alive in well-researched settings. Having lived in Germany the first half of her life and the second half in various parts of the U.S., Oppenlander inspires readers by illuminating story questions as relevant today as they were in the past.

Oppenlander shares her knowledge through writing workshops at colleges, libraries and schools. She also offers vivid presentations and author visits. The mother of fraternal twins and a son, she recently moved with her husband and old mutt, Mocha, to Solingen, Germany.

"Nearly every place holds some kind of secret, something that makes history come alive. When we scrutinize people and places closely, history is no longer a date or number, it turns into a story."

*Thank you for reading 47 DAYS. My sincere hope is that you derived as much entertainment from reading this story as I enjoyed in creating it. If you have a few moments, please feel free to add your review of the book at your favorite online site for feedback (Amazon, Apple iTunes Store, Goodreads, etc.). Also, if you would like to connect with previous or upcoming books, please visit my website for information and to sign up for e-news: https://www.annetteoppenlander.com.*

*Sincerely, Annette*

# CONTACT ME

I always love to hear from you! Please don't hesitate to drop me a note via the website contact form or on Facebook.

Website: www.annetteoppenlander.com
Facebook: www.facebook.com/annetteoppenlanderauthor
Twitter: @aoppenlander
Pinterest: @annoppenlander

# ABOUT THIS NOVELETTE

47 DAYS is an excerpt from the novel, SURVING THE FATHERLAND, a sweeping saga of family, love, and betrayal against the epic panorama of WWII which illuminates an intimate part of history seldom seen: the children's war. Spanning thirteen years from 1940 until 1953, SURVIVING THE FATHERLAND tells the stories of Günter and Lilly struggling with the terror-filled reality of life in the Third Reich, each embarking on their own dangerous path toward survival, freedom, and ultimately each other. Based on the author's own family and anchored in historical facts, this story celebrates the resilience of the human spirit and the strength of war children.

# AWARDS AND REVIEWS
## 'SURVIVING THE FATHERLAND'

2017 National Indie Excellence Award
2018 Indie B.R.A.G. Award
2017 Winner Chill with a Book Readers' Award
Finalist 2017 Kindle Book Awards
2018 Readers' Favorite Book Award
Discovered Diamond Historical Novel
2019 Global eBook Award Gold
An IWIC Hall of Fame Novel
2020 Skoutz-Award Midlist (Germany)

"This book needs to join the ranks of the classic survivor stories of
WWII such as "Diary of Anne Frank" and "Man's Search for
Meaning". It is truly that amazing!" **InD'tale Magazine**

"This novel is fast-paced and emotively worded and features a
great selection of characters, flawed and poignantly three-
dimensional." **Historical Novel Society**

"...eye-opening and heartbreaking..." **San Francisco Review of
Books**

"I would heartily recommend this book as an engrossing and well-
researched story with two of the most engaging protagonists I've

read for a while." Jessica Brown for **Discovering Diamonds - Independent Reviews of the Best in Historical Fiction**

"I for one am glad she shared her story with us as it gives us a look at a different perspective from those who endured this tragic time in history. "Surviving the Fatherland" by Annette Oppenlander is highly recommended reading!" Carol Hoyer for **Reader Views**

"…simply beautiful." **Readers' Favorite Five Stars**

PREVIEW


SURVIVING THE FATHERLAND
A True Coming-of-age Love Story
Set in WWII Germany


CHAPTER ONE


**Lilly: May 1940**

For me the war began, not with Hitler's invasion of Poland, but with my father's lie. I was seven at the time, a skinny thing with pigtails and bony knees, dressed in my mother's lumpy hand-knitted sweaters, a girl who loved her father more than anything.

It was May of 1940, my favorite time of year when the air is filled with the smell of cut grass and lilacs, promising excursions to town and the cafes in the hilly land I called home.

Like any other weekend, my father came home that Friday carrying a heavy briefcase of folders. Only this time, he flung his case in the corner of the hallway like it was a bag of garbage. You have to understand. My father is a neat freak, a man who keeps himself and everything he touches in absolute order. And so even at seven—even before he said those fateful words—I knew something was different.

My father had been named after the German emperor, Wilhelm, and Mutti called him Willi, but to me he was always Vati.

Ignoring me, he hurried into the kitchen, his eyes bright with excitement. "I've been drafted."

At the sink, Mutti abruptly dropped her sponge and stared at him. Her mouth opened, then closed without a sound.

I didn't understand what he was talking about. I didn't understand the meaning of a lie, yet I felt it even then. Like others detect an oncoming thunderstorm, pressure builds behind my forehead, a heaviness in my bones. There is something in the way the liar moves, his limbs hang stiffly on the body as if his soul cringes. His look at me is fleeting and there is something artificial in his voice.

At that moment I knew Vati was hiding something from us.

"They want me there Monday. I'll be a major." His voice trembled as he sank into a chair, still wearing his coat and hat.

"But that's in three days." Mutti picked up Burkhart, my little brother who was a just a toddler and had begun to whine. "It's fine," she soothed as she paced the length of the kitchen, the click-click of her heels like an accusation.

I frowned and moved closer to my father. Since my brother's birth, Mutti had been spending every minute with the baby. No matter how well I behaved, how I did what she asked, I rarely succeeded drawing her eyes away from my brother. It annoyed me to no end that I couldn't stop myself from trying.

"Vati, where are you going?" I asked, secure in the knowledge that my little brother wouldn't draw away his attention.

My father cheeks glowed with excitement. As if he hadn't heard me, he rushed back into the hallway and knelt in front of the wardrobe. I followed.

One door gaped open, revealing a gray military uniform. He was rummaging below.

"What are you looking for?"

"Just a minute." He emerged with a pair of shiny black boots.

He knelt at my level and to this day I remember smelling the cologne he used every morning, a mix of spice and citrus.

"I am packing."

"Where are you going?" Vati had never been away, not

even for one night. In fact, he and Mutti had strict routines, and these were dictated by the clock. We ate every night at six thirty sharp. Even on Sundays. Breakfast was at seven in the morning. Clothes never ever lay on the floor, each item brushed and aired and returned to its spot in the closet. Life was laid out in rules, washing hands before dinner, carrying a clean handkerchief at all times and always, always looking spotless when leaving the house.

He smoothed the pants of his uniform. "I'll be helping out in the war."

"Will you be back for my birthday?" My birthday was on June fourth and I worried about our customary visits to town. In the window of *Wiesner*, our local toy store, I'd discovered a *Schildkröt* doll. Her name was Inge and I wanted her badly. Vati said she looked just like me, with blond hair and this pretty red-checkered dress with a white apron and white patent shoes you could take off.

As Vati lifted me in the air and turned in a circle, I shrieked in surprise and delight. I was flying.

"They want me after all! With all my experience, they should be glad."

Mutti put Burkhart on the floor and leaned in the doorframe to the kitchen, her arms folded across her chest. "I wish you didn't have to go."

"It's not so bad, Luise." Vati gripped her shoulders as if he wanted to infuse his excitement into her. "I'll be back soon. We're so much stronger than last time."

"All I see is Hitler sending more men into battle. Do you at least know where you're going?"

Vati shrugged. "Probably France or Scandinavia."

"Will you be back soon?" I tried again.

He patted my head and returned to his chair at the head of the table. "I'll be home before you've found time to miss me." As he began to whistle, something nagged my insides like a tiny clawing animal.

A screeching wail erupted. Sharp and metallic, it cut through doors and walls and echoed through the streets. No matter that the siren blasted every day, it made me shiver.

I watched my mother freeze, her eyes filled with something I would soon learn to recognize as fear. The siren continued—up, down, up, down. Another wail erupted. This time it sounded like the foghorn of a ship, signaling the end of the alarm.

Relieved that the horrible noise was over, I climbed on my father's lap, running a forefinger across the bluish stubble of his jaw. "Vati?"

"Not now, Lieselotte, we are talking," Mutti said.

I looked up in alarm. Mutti had said Lieselotte when everyone called me Lilly, a sure sign she was mad. I slid back off, keeping my hand on Vati's arm.

Mutti tucked a strand of pale hair behind her ear and slumped into a chair. "I hate these air raid sirens."

Vati didn't look up from the newspaper. "It's just a test… a precaution."

Mutti abruptly straightened. "I should work on dinner. You *do* remember that my brother is visiting tonight?" Two red spots that didn't quite match her lipstick glowed on her cheeks. "Lilly, there's honey all over this table. Wash out the dishrag and wipe this down."

"Yes, Mutti." I clumsily scrubbed the surface, glancing back and forth between my parents. Vati's eyes, usually a watery blue, sparkled like an early morning sky.

"Don't you see that this is important?" he said, letting the paper sink once more. "We're fighting against England and France, even Scandinavia! Our country needs us."

"You mean they need you."

"Everyone has a role to play."

"They didn't ask me if *I* wanted to play a role." Mutti's voice was shrill as she set a pot on the stove and began to peel potatoes. "I'll be stuck with two children to take care of."

"That's exactly what the Führer wants you to do. Girls are meant to be mothers and take care of our families. We take care of the rest."

"Like your war?"

Hearing my parents argue made my insides turn knotty. I wanted them to stop, yet I finished cleaning and said nothing. All I did was return to Vati's chair as their arguments continued flying like knives above my head.

"We have to make sacrifices," Vati said. "You're a strong woman. Besides, isn't the government taking care of things? Every family receives rations, even for clothes. They're thinking of everything."

"These ration cards are so cumbersome. And the sirens drive me crazy."

Vati got up and patted Mutti's back. "Don't worry, everything will work out fine.

During dinner, I continued watching my parents. Heavy silence lingered except for my brother's babble and the scraping of spoons across porcelain bowls.

I didn't taste much of the soup. My eyes were drawn to the stony faces on either side as I recalled the events of the afternoon, wondering if I had done something to make them angry. In that stillness of the kitchen, I sensed that my life was about to change. Something dreadful lingered like a wolf lying in wait behind a bush ready to pounce. You didn't see it or hear it, yet you knew it was there.

"Tim says that women who wear lipstick are whores," I said, my gaze lingering on my mother's mouth where the remnants of lipstick clung to her lower lip.

"Who is Tim?" Mutti snapped.

"A boy in my class. His older brother is in the Hitler youth and they say girls should not paint their faces and listen to the men—"

"Young girls like yourself are pretty just the way they are," Vati said.

I was sure Tim had talked about all women and though I burned to know what a whore was, I decided to keep my mouth shut. My teacher's probing eyes appeared in my vision, and I remembered my earlier mission.

"Vati, will you read with me tonight?" I was a terrible reader, hated it, especially when I had to read aloud in class and Herr Poll slammed his ruler on my desk when I got stuck.

Mutti's mouth pressed together in a straight line as she headed for the window to pull down the blackout shutters. "Not tonight," she said. "Clear the table while I cover the other windows and change your brother. Then you get ready for bed."

Vati jumped up and disappeared in the living room. "We'll do it another time," he said before he closed the door.

As I watched Mutti carry Burkhart to bed, I felt as transparent as the air around me. But not in a comfortable way— more like a sore throat that sticks around and reminds you off and on that you're still sick.

After stacking our dishes in the sink, I followed my father, who was studying a file of papers.

"Vati?"

"What is it, Lilly?"

I hesitated. Was this a good time to ask about *Inge*, the doll? Vati was acting so strange. Even now his face had a damp shine to it as if he'd run to catch the streetcar.

"Nothing," I said. *Gute Nacht*, Vati."

"Sweet dreams."

Disappointed, I quietly closed the door, stopping halfway to my bedroom. No sounds came from the kitchen.

I was about to climb into bed when the doorbell rang. I froze. Something bad was going to happen. Was the war coming to get Vati?

But when I heard voices in the corridor I recognized Mutti's brother, August, my favorite uncle. He always brought me gifts, a chocolate éclair, a flower from his garden or a bowl of sweet cherries.

I breathed again, growing aware of my icy feet on the linoleum.

By the sounds they'd gone into the living room, a perfect opportunity to see my uncle and find out more about Vati's plans. If I pretended my stomach ached, maybe, just maybe I could visit for a while. I bent over my brother who was lying on his back, his mouth relaxed in sleep, blonde curls framing his face. In that moment I envied him. It wouldn't be the last time.

On the other side of the wall, Vati shouted. Alarmed, I tiptoed into the hallway and peeked through the living room door. Uncle August, his legs stretched long in front of him, lounged on the sofa next to a young woman I didn't recognize, while Mutti sat on an armchair by the window.

"I don't believe this. How can you be so enthusiastic?" August's voice rose as he spoke, at the same time patting the young woman's knee. "Don't you remember the last war? You of all people."

"Nonsense," Vati said from somewhere beyond the door. "This war will be over quickly. Our weapons are superior. I mean, Poland practically fell in a day and France and Scandinavia aren't far behind."

August shook his head, his eyes squinting. "I don't understand how you turn your back on your family." His voice was filled with disgust. "Aren't you worried about leaving your wife and children? This damn thing gives me the creeps. The SS and Gestapo are watching our every step. Just the other day—"

"Shhh," the woman next to him said. "August, please be careful. What if somebody listens?"

"I'm not turning my back," Vati shouted. "We've got to do our duty. Besides, the Führer is taking care of everyone."

August threw a glance at Mutti. "Since when can we trust the government?"

Mutti leaned forward. "The apartment below is vacant. When Willi leaves, I won't even have a neighbor to talk to," she choked, her eyes glistening. "You want me to ask Herr Baum? He's older than Methuselah and can barely walk, let alone help if things get worse."

I cringed. I liked the old man next door, especially his knobby hands that were brown and gnarled like miniature tree trunks. He always listened when I spoke as if what I said were important.

"I'm convinced this war will be over before the year is up." Vati sounded irritated, and there was that darkness again, that fakeness in his voice. "I, for my part, am proud to help out."

August jumped up so suddenly, I nearly banged my head against the doorframe. "Well, I'm not." His eyes narrowed. "I thought your job at the city was highly important. Strange they let their top civil engineer walk off like that."

The silence that followed reminded me of dinner when my parents hadn't spoken, yet I could hear their anger as clearly as if they'd screamed at each other. I no longer wanted to go inside, yet I couldn't leave, my legs as rigid as Herr Poll's ruler.

"Either way," August continued, "all I wanted was to introduce my fiancée, Annelise. I'm sorry I came."

Mutti stood up, wiping her eyes. "Please August, don't go yet. I'm sure it'll all work out."

"That's right," Vati said, sounding calm again. "Let's drink to your engagement. I'll get a bottle of wine from the cellar."

I rushed to my bedroom and curled up tightly the way I did during thunderstorms. It took me another hour to get to sleep, my mind firmly on the image of Vati handing me the doll, Inge, for my birthday.

# CHAPTER TWO

**Günter: May 1940**

"Attention! Feet together, arms down, hands at your pant seams. Look straight. Stand still," the boy shouted. He was no more than sixteen, and the khaki uniform hung in folds around his narrow chest. The hair around his ears, shaved to the skin, left a tuft of blonde on top like a bird's nest.

He paced up and down in front of us, a row of eleven year-old boys, his eyes narrowed into angry slits. "Men," he yelled, "you are the future soldiers of Germany. You don't fight to die, but to win." He yanked open a book. "I quote. Nothing is more important than your courage. Only the strong person, carried by belief and the fighting desire of your own blood, will be master during danger." The book snapped shut. "I expect absolute obedience."

I stood next to my best friend, Helmut, at the sports stadium where the local Hitler youth met for drill. We'd lined up in rows of three deep in the middle of the grass-covered field. Another boy with red and blue patches on his shirt appeared in front of us.

"Tuck in your shirt, pull up your socks," he said, pointing at Helmut. "Look at the filth on your shoes. This is no way to dress. Show some pride."

From the corner of my eye, I watched Helmut adjust his shirt and rub his shoes. Helmut sometimes forgets about these things. Thankfully my own socks stretched to just below my knees.

71

Still, I held my breath as the boy passed by. Earlier today we'd bought a uniform: black shorts and beige shirt, neckerchief with leather knot, armband, and the best part, a brand-new knife. Mother had grumbled about spending so much money.

"But Mutter, all boys have to go," I'd argued after we left the store. "They told us at school. It's our duty." I didn't tell her how excited I'd been about my new outfit. Most of the time I get the hand-me-downs from my older brother, Hans.

"What're they going to do with you?" she'd said, her voice stern with irritation.

"Make fires and camp." I didn't tell Mother that I couldn't wait trying out my new knife and going on adventures with a bunch of boys.

Now I waited in a line and couldn't move a muscle. Stupid.

"Attention! Turn left, march! One, two, one, two, follow me." Birdsnest headed down the field while the other youth observed, waiting for us to trip and fall out of line. We marched back and forth, left and right, crisscrossing the field. What a bore.

The air smelled of early summer and warmth. Dandelions and forget-me-nots dotted the grass like a colorful carpet. Imitating my classmates, I fought the urge to look around, keeping my head straight toward the horizon as if I could see what was coming a mile away.

A man in a brown uniform with a red armband watched from the sidelines. Distracted for a moment, I stepped on the heels of the fellow in front.

"Ouch," the boy yelled. "Watch yourself, idiot."

"You're the idiot. Why did you stop?" I said.

Birdsnest materialized in front of us. "What's going on here?"

"He stepped on me," the other boy said.

My cheeks felt hot. "He suddenly stopped."

"Name."

"What?"

"Your *name*."

"Günter Schmidt."

"Listen to me, Günter." Birdsnest's eyes narrowed. "Quit playing around. You're training to become a soldier. On the ground. Give me twenty pushups, quick."

"Yes, sir." I hurriedly dropped to the grass and hid my face because my head had turned into a super-heated balloon ready to fly away.

Out of breath I returned to the row, swallowing the choice words choking me. The marching continued, followed by singing:

*"Our flag flies in front of us;*
*To the future we trek man for man,*
*We march for Hitler through night and adversity*
*With the youth's flag for freedom and bread.*
*Our flag flies in front of us,*
*Our flag is the new era,*
*Our flag leads us into eternity,*
*Yes, the flag is more than death.*

Birdsnest continued reading from his book about becoming heroes, but my thoughts, sped up by the gnawing in my stomach, wandered to the dinner waiting at home. On dismissal, Birdsnest gave me a nasty look before reminding us to practice marching and standing to attention. He never mentioned camping or making fires. *Boring.* We weren't allowed to use our knives either. Worse, we'd have to go again Saturday.

By the time I arrived at my house, it was late and I was in a rotten mood. Helmut is much more of a talker, but he was grumpy, too, and we'd walked home in silence.

I lived on the first floor of an apartment house on *Weinsbergtalstrasse*, one of a row of identical three-story homes. Recently built of brick and stucco, they were considered modern, each house painted the same pale green except for an occasional flower box in a white-framed window. I loved our new water closet. You pulled on the chain, which I was strictly forbidden to play with, and the water released from a tank under the ceiling, flushing everything away. Helmut still had an outhouse.

Entering our flat, I tossed my cap in the corner and headed to the kitchen. "I'm hom—"

The words stuck in my throat because the table, set for five, was untouched, the room deserted. A sense of unease crept up inside me, quickly forgotten because of the delicious smell emanating from the cast-iron pot. I lifted the lid and let out a sigh: bean soup with ham and smoked sausage. I glanced at the clock, seven-thirty. No wonder I was starving.

We never ate later than six. Something was wrong.

Reluctantly, I turned away from the soup and tiptoed down the hallway. Voices came from my parents' bedroom.

Stopping at the threshold, I knocked. "*Vater?*"

"Come in."

I cracked open the door. "Are we going to eat?"

Mother sat hunched over on the bed, my father kneeling in front of her. I wanted to enter, but something in their expressions held me back.

My father straightened with effort. "I'm leaving tomorrow."

"What do you mean?" I looked back and forth between my parents.

"I've been drafted."

I stared at him as his words echoed through my head. "But you said they needed you in the factory. You said you had more work than you could handle, making those fancy swords for the officers."

"That's what I thought." My father's voice remained steady but his jaws were tight.

"Can't you tell them you're too busy?"

My father sighed and put an arm on my shoulder, his expression serious. Despite being short, he could carry a hundred kilo sack of grain as if it were a small child. He wasn't the hugging type, but tonight he held on to me.

"That's not how it works."

"Where will you go?"

"Don't know. Maybe to Scandinavia."

Wiping her eyes, Mother stood up. "Why don't you get your brothers and eat? We'll pack and be in soon. And take off those clothes."


During the night, despite being tired, I tossed and turned. I'd burned my tongue on the soup at dinner, and my stomach was making weird noises. By the sound of it, my older brother, Hans, wasn't sleeping either.

While the radio proclaimed victories daily, news of fallen soldiers had begun to arrive, and announcements appeared in the newspaper. A square black cross was printed above each obituary and Mother grumbled and shook her head, reading the names and ages of the dead. I envisioned my father stumbling blindly toward a sea of barbwire, his head and eyes wrapped in bandages, his arms stretched in front.

Time stood still in the early morning hours as I wondered if my father would return with limbs missing or not at all. I imagined the obituary in the paper: Artur Schmidt, died in battle. I considered asking Hans what he thought would happen, but before I could, a soft snore came from the other bed.

I turned on my back and stared into the darkness. The apartment was silent, but not the silence of peaceful sleep, rather an artificial stillness of cries muffled by pillows and of thoughts that whirled without end. I turned again, facing the wall, my last thought of my father waving to me with a rifle.

In the morning I awoke with a start. My brother's bed was a pile of sheets and blankets. Remembering last night, I sighed. Soft murmurs drifted in from the kitchen—my father's voice. I wanted to stay in bed and listen, and at the same time I wanted to be near him.

With a sigh, I jumped out of bed.

"Günter, you sleepy head." My father opened his arms. "Give me a hug."

I buried my face in the folds of my father's shirt. "Are you leaving now?" My father smelled of shaving soap, reminding me of his ritual, the razor, a single sharp blade, swiped back and forth across a leather strap to sharpen it further, the soft foamy soap and the thick brush made of badger hair, my father disappearing under a layer of white bubbles before taking the knife to scrape away the stubble.

"It's time."

Everybody crowded in. I sobbed, my throat tight and achy.

My father grabbed me and Hans by the arm. "You two need to take care of your mother and Siegfried."

I swallowed hard, the lump in my throat threatening to expand to my eyes. I knew that Hans was upset by the way his shoulders trembled. My baby brother, Siegfried, was only three and had no idea what was going on.

"I don't want to hear of any mischief. Do what you're told."

"Yes, *Vater*," I said. "When will you come back?"

"As soon as they let me."

"Promise?"

"I'll write." My father moved toward Mother. "I'll see you soon, Grete," he whispered.

Wiping his eyes with the back of his hand, he turned. For a moment he looked around the living room, the leather sofa, his favorite chair in the corner, the walnut table and matching sideboard.

A bright morning sun beamed into the room, throwing patterns on the wood. A starling trilled high of summer and new beginnings. With a final nod, my father hurried to the door—and was gone.

Mother dabbed her eyes where fresh tears kept arriving. "You heard what your father said. We better talk about your new responsibilities."

"Can't we do it after school?" My legs were heavy from lack of sleep.

Mother resolutely picked up pen and paper. "Who wants to help with laundry?"

"That's girl's work," Hans said. "Besides, I'm too old for that."

"Not me," I said.

"Enough." Mother smacked a fist on the table. And though she was a short woman and even at eleven I was taller than her, I bowed my head. "You heard what your father said. Günter, you'll help with laundry. Hans, you'll do the ovens. I also need someone to clean the hallway stairs and sweep the sidewalk." I tuned out.

Life was going to be one big chore.

End of Chapter Two

Made in the USA
Las Vegas, NV
02 December 2022